Heidi's Irresistible Hat

WRITTEN BY ELIZABETH CRARY ▪ ILLUSTRATED BY SUSAN AVISHAI

Parenting Press, Inc.

SEATTLE, WASHINGTO

D1366802

Parenting Press, Inc.
P.O. Box 75267, Seattle, Washington 98125
www.ParentingPress.com

First edition
Printed in the United States of America

Book design by Margarite Hargrave

Library of Congress Cataloging-in-Publication Data

Crary, Elizabeth, 1942-
    Heidi's irresistible hat / written by Elizabeth Crary ; illustrated by Susan Avishai.
        p. cm. -- (A kids can choose book)
    ISBN 1-884734-56-1 (lib. bdg.) – ISBN 1-884734-55-3 (pbk.)
        1. Problem solving in children–Juvenile literature. 2. Teasing–Juvenile literature.
    [1. Problem solving. 2. Teasing.] I. Avishai, Susan, ill. II. Title.

BF723.P8 C725 2001
153.4'3–dc21   00-062380

Note to Parents, Teachers, and Caregivers

When a child faces a frustrating situation, the more ideas he or she considers, the more appropriate his or her behavior is likely to be.

The "Kids Can Choose" books model a process for solving problems and offer a variety of ways children can respond. Each book in this series explores a common problem for children, such as nonviolent teasing, theft of personal belongings, and personal space encroachment.

In each story some choices are successful and others are not–this helps children realize that they may need to try *several* strategies before they find one that works. The characters also model reflecting on various options *before they act.*

How to Use These Books

Read the story and let your child make the choices. When you come to a box (■) read the question and wait while your child responds. Accept his or her responses without correction or criticism. You can ask your child to elaborate with questions like "Why do you think that worked?" or "Have you ever tried something like that?"

Transition from Story to Real Life

It takes more than reading these books several times for children to be able to *apply* the principles to real life. Children need to practice using the approach in non-stressful situations. The following five steps make the transfer easier:

1. Act out the situation in the book with other kids or adults.
2. Brainstorm new ideas and add them to the list on page 30.
3. Pick five ideas (one for each finger) and act them out with an imaginary problem.
4. Choose five ideas for a past problem and act them out.
5. Ask your child to list different ways to handle a current problem and act them out.

When children can use the approach in non-stressful situations, you can remind them they have options in real life. For example, you could say, "What options have you considered?" or, for children who are reluctant to talk about their issues, "What might Heidi have done in a situation like yours?"

Through these books you are helping your child learn to make smart decisions. Keep the tone light and *have fun!*

Elizabeth Crary
Seattle, Washington

Heidi pulled her hat down over her ears. It was her favorite hat. Aunt Sarah had made it just for her. Heidi liked the way the point on top stood straight up when she pulled the hat on.

Heidi put her jacket on, too, for it was now cool in the crisp October mornings. With a "good-bye" to Mom, she started off toward school. It was fun to walk through fallen leaves. Heidi wished she didn't have to go to school today though. It wasn't that her teacher was mean. She was really fun. It wasn't that the other girls were mean. She had lots of fun with them, too. The problem was her hat.

"Well," Heidi thought, "not my hat, really. The problem is that Paul always takes my hat."

Everyday when she got to school, Paul would snatch her hat off and wave it around out of her reach. When she would ask for it back, he would laugh and toss it to someone else. Eventually, he would give it back to her, but not until the school bell rang.

When she told her dad about Paul, he said, "Sometimes boys tease girls they like. Best to just ignore him."

"Easy for you to say," Heidi grumbled as she thought about trying to ignore Paul. "Maybe I'll just grab my hat back. Or better yet, maybe I'll grab his hat!"

As soon as Heidi entered the playground, Paul appeared as if by magic and snatched her hat. "Give me my hat!" Heidi demanded. Paul grinned and danced away, waving her hat in the air.

Heidi was so mad she wanted to cry. "What can I do?" she wondered. Several ideas flashed in her mind.

■ What do you think Heidi will try first?

(Wait for child to respond after each question. Look at page 3, "Note to Parents, Teachers, and Caregivers," for ways to encourage children to think for themselves.)

10 Ask Paul to give back her hat

"What should I do?" Heidi wondered. "Shall I grab my hat back or tell on Paul? The teacher always says to ask for what you want before you do anything rash. So maybe I should ask. Maybe he'll give my hat back to me if I ask."

She stood up straight and walked toward Paul. He backed away. She called to him, "Paul, please give me my hat back."

"What hat?" he said as he hid her hat behind his back.

"The one behind your back," she replied.

"I don't have a hat behind my back," he said as he tossed her hat to a friend.

"Hey, that wasn't nice. I asked you to give me my hat, and you threw it to someone else. That really makes me mad."

■ What do you think Heidi will try next?

12 Grab her hat back

Heidi decided to grab her hat back. She ran after Paul. He continued to hold the hat out of her reach, waving it around, and chanting, "I got your ha-at. I got your ha-at."

"Give it to me!" Heidi demanded.

Paul continued to wave it about, chanting, "I have your ha-at. I have your ha-at."

Heidi reached up. She almost grabbed the hat, but Paul moved away slightly. She tried again. He moved away again.

Heidi jumped up. She touched her hat and then lost her balance and fell. Paul danced away with her hat.

She wasn't hurt, but she was very mad. So mad she wanted to explode. She wanted her hat, but didn't know how to get it back.

■ What do you think Heidi will try next?

14 Ignore Paul

Heidi decided to ignore Paul.

She remembered what her dad said, "Ignoring means not responding. Don't look. Don't listen. Stand tall. Pretend he's disappeared in a puff of smoke and you have your hat."

"Well," Heidi said, straightening up tall. "I guess I can try ignoring." As she looked for her friend Jenny, Paul danced closer and chanted, "I have your ha-at. I have your ha-at."

"Don't listen. Pretend you don't hear," Heidi reminded herself as her stomach churned. She stood up on her toes, looking around for Jenny. She continued to ignore Paul's chanting. "Don't listen. Don't listen," she repeated to herself.

Just as she saw Jenny, the bell rang. Paul tossed Heidi her hat and ran in. Heidi picked up her hat and wondered if it was worth it. Ignoring was hard work.

"Next time Paul takes my hat, maybe I'll try something else," she thought.

■ What do you think Heidi will try next?

16 Decide it's no big deal

"Am I making trouble for myself?" Heidi wondered, as Paul waved her hat around. "Dad said Paul takes my hat because he likes me. That sounds dumb. Paul always gives it back, though.

"Mom says that you can always see things in different ways, like a glass of water half empty or half full. Or like yesterday, when she reminded me I could be happy with one cookie or disappointed I didn't have two.

"If Mom and Dad are both right, then I don't have to worry. Paul will return my hat. I can play until then without worrying.

"Okay, I'll try," she decided. She gave Paul a smile and ran off toward her friends. He followed her, waving the hat.

Heidi concentrated on talking with Jenny and Maria. "This is interesting," Heidi thought. "Changing how I see things is a little like ignoring, but easier since I believe it will be okay."

After a bit, Paul tossed her the hat and headed back to his friends.
The End

■ How do you like this ending?

18 Get more ideas

"Nothing works. Ignoring's impossible. Asking doesn't work. And grabbing it back is hopeless," Heidi grumbled to herself. "I need more ideas."

During recess, she joined her friends. "Paul grabs my hat when I come to school. I can't make him stop. What can I do?" she asked.

"You can grab his hat and show him how it feels," Kate said quickly.

"You could tie your hat on so when he pulls it doesn't come off. I did that so my brother couldn't get my cap, and it really worked," Jenny added.

"What you really need," Marie interjected, "is a special wall to keep Paul away."

"I know," interrupted Jenny, "we can be a walking wall and protect Heidi's hat. We could start tomorrow."

■ What do you think Heidi will try next?

20 Make a walking wall

When she got up the next morning, Heidi thought to herself, "I do need help." As she waited for her friends to arrive, she reviewed her plan. "If they walk around me, Paul won't be able to get close enough to take my hat." She hoped the plan would really protect her hat.

When she was getting ready for school, she told her mom that she was going to walk to school with several friends.

Soon everyone was at her house. They walked together until they got to the school, then the other girls formed a box around Heidi. It felt funny to be in the middle, sort of like being part of a marching band.

Paul watched as they crossed the playground to the school building. He looked puzzled. What were they up to?

Heidi put her jacket and hat in her locker. She gave her friends a high five and went to class smiling. "Finally, I didn't have to fight over my hat," she thought with satisfaction.

The End

■ How do you like this ending?

22 Get help from a grown-up

Heidi decided to ask the playground monitor for help. "Mrs. Bennet, Paul took my hat and won't give it back. He did that yesterday and the day before, too. Please help me."

"What have you tried?" Mrs. Bennet asked.

"I've tried asking for my hat back, grabbing it, and ignoring him. But nothing works. He holds my hat out of reach or tosses it to a friend," Heidi explained.

Mrs. Bennet called Paul over and asked, "Did you take Heidi's hat today?"

"Well, sort of, but it was for fun," Paul replied.

"Was it fun for Heidi?" Mrs. Bennet asked.

"I guess not," Paul answered.

"I want you to return her hat and apologize. You need to ask someone before you take something that's not yours."

"Oh, all right. I'm sorry I upset you, Heidi." Paul said reluctantly, as he gave Heidi her hat.

The End

■ How do you like this ending?

24 Do the unexpected

Heidi stared at her hat. "What can I do so that Paul can't get my hat off?" she wondered. "Tying a ribbon around my head to hold it on would look stupid. Hair clips won't hold very well. . . . I know, I can use a button and loop. If I make a strong loop and sew a button real tight, it should work."

First, she found a bright blue button and sewed it on her hat. Then she got some strong yarn and threaded three strands through the hat. She braided them until the string was long enough to go around the button, then tied it off. Now she had a button and a loop.

The next morning Heidi was excited to go to school. She wondered if Paul would try to snatch her hat again. She almost wished he would, so she could test her idea.

When she got to school, sure enough, Paul came over and tried to pluck her hat off. When it didn't fall, he tried pulling on it, but it stayed on. Paul frowned and said, "What did you do? Glue it to your head?"

Heidi nodded, and then added, "That way I won't lose it."

The End

■ How do you like this ending?

26 Change her schedule

"How can I keep Paul from grabbing my hat?" Heidi muttered to herself. "As soon as I get to school, he takes my hat.

"If I'm not there, Paul can't grab my hat. But I would get in trouble for skipping school. I could pretend to be sick, but then I'd miss my friends.

"Maybe I could go later, but I might be tardy, and then I would have to miss recess.... There must be something I can do," she thought.

"I know what I can do. I can help the librarian," she smiled.

The next morning she got up early. She told her mom she was going early to help Mrs. Sanchez, the librarian.

As she put books away in the library, she glanced out the window. She could see Paul playing by the gate. Occasionally, he would look down the street, but Heidi knew her hat was safe.

The End

■ How do you like this ending?

28 Do something funny

Being mad felt yucky. Heidi took several deep breaths so she could calm down. After a few minutes she was calm.

"What can I do that will be kind of funny?" Heidi wondered as Paul tossed her hat into the air.

Suddenly, she remembered the ball game her dad was watching the night before. The announcer was describing what happened to the ball, play-by-play.

Quickly, she pulled her umbrella from her pocket. Using it as a micro-phone, she began a commentary.

"Number 2 snatched the hat from number 1. He marks time by tossing the hat in the air from hand to hand. He makes a daring toss way, way up and barely catches it. Number 2 tosses the hat to number 3. Number 3 grabs the hat and tosses it over the head of number 1 back to number 2. . . . "

Soon, everyone was giggling. Someone tossed the hat to Heidi, she grabbed it, and announced, "That's all for now, folks," as she put the hat on and the umbrella back in her pocket. Everybody dashed into the school building as the bell rang.

The End

■ How do you like this ending?

Idea page

Heidi's ideas

■ Ask Paul to give back her hat

■ Grab her hat back

■ Ignore Paul

■ Decide it's no big deal

■ Get more ideas

■ Make a walking wall

■ Get help from a grown-up

■ Do the unexpected

■ Change her schedule

■ Do something funny

Your ideas

■

■

■

■

■

■

■

■

■

■

■

■

■

■

Solving social problems...

Children's Problem Solving Books teach children to think about their problems. Each interactive story allows the reader to choose the main character's actions and see what happens as a result. Useful with 3–8 years. 32 pages, illustrated. $6.95 each. Written by Elizabeth Crary, illustrated by Marina Megale.

Solving interpersonal problems...

Kids Can Choose Books teach children to think about problems they may have with other children. Each interactive story allows the reader to choose the main character's actions and see what happens as a result. Useful with 5-10 years. 32 pages, illustrated. $7.95 each. Written by Elizabeth Crary, illustrated by Susan Avishai.

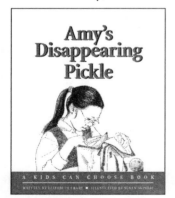

Someone is stealing Amy's pickle. What can she do?

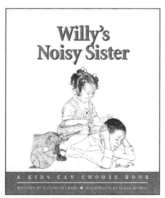

Willy needs some peace and quiet. His sister wants to play–NOW! What can he do?

One of Heidi's classmates always snatches her hat off her head. What can she do?

Coping with intense feelings . . .

Dealing with Feelings Books acknowledge six intense feelings. Children discover safe and creative ways to express them. Each interactive story allows the reader to choose the main character's actions and see what happens as a result. Useful with 3-9 years. 32 pages, illustrated. $6.95 each. Written by Elizabeth Crary, illustrated by Jean Whitney.

Facing life's challenges . . .

The Decision Is Yours Books offer realistic dilemmas commonly faced by young people. Readers choose from among several alternatives to solve the problem. If they don't like the result of one solution, they can try a different one. Useful with 7-11 years. 64 pages, illustrated. $5.95 each. Various authors, illustrated by Rebekah Strecker.

Leader's Guide ($14.95) written by Carl Bosch offers activities that allow children to talk about values, ethics, feelings, safety, problem solving, and understanding behavior.

Library-bound editions available. Call Parenting Press, Inc. at **1-800-992-6657** for information about these and other helpful books for children and adults.

Prices subject to change without notice.